*A*my March wants to be a great artist. She's got the talent; now all she needs is a way to afford art lessons. Her solution: befriend her rich and snobby classmate, Jenny Snow, who'll then invite Amy to sit in on her private art instruction. But Jenny can't be bothered with Amy's friendly overtures — until Diana Hughes, a new and extremely wealthy girl, chooses Amy as her friend. Now Amy thinks Jenny will like her too. But the price for art lessons may be higher than Amy ever imagined. . . .

PORTRAITS
of LITTLE WOMEN

Amy Makes
a Friend

Don't miss any of the
Portraits of Little Women

PORTRAITS
of LITTLE WOMEN
Amy Makes
a Friend

Susan Beth Pfeffer

DELACORTE PRESS

Published by
Delacorte Press
Bantam Doubleday Dell Publishing Group, Inc.
1540 Broadway
New York, New York 10036

Library of Congress Cataloging-in-Publication Data
Pfeffer, Susan Beth.
    Portraits of Little Women, Amy makes a friend / Susan Beth Pfeffer.
       p.   cm.
    "Inspired by Louisa May Alcott's Little Women."
    Summary: Desperate for art lessons, Amy hopes to manipulate her
friendship with two other girls to get what she wants.
    ISBN 0-385-32584-3
    [1. Friendship—Fiction. 2. Artists—Fiction. 3. Sisters—Fiction.
4. Family life—New England—Fiction. 5. New England—Fiction.]
I. Alcott, Louisa May, 1832–1888. Little women. II. Title.
PZ7.P44855Pif   1998
[Fic]—dc21   97-49508
                                               CIP
                                               AC

The text of this book is set in 13-point Cochin.

Cover and text design by Patrice Sheridan
Cover illustration copyright © 1998 by Lori Earley
Text illustrations copyright © 1998 by Marcy Ramsey
Activities illustrations copyright © 1998 by Laura Maestro

Manufactured in the United States of America

July 1998

10 9 8 7 6 5 4 3 2 1

BVG

FOR ANNE WEBER

CONTENTS

CHAPTER 1

*A*my March looked at the sketch she had just drawn of her sisters and frowned. She wanted to crumple the paper and throw it away, but she couldn't afford to. Paper cost money, and since money was scarce in the March household, Amy knew she should draw another picture on the back of the first one. Still, Amy was sure great artists didn't use both sides of their sketchpads. Not great *rich* artists, at least.

"Let me see," said Amy's oldest sister, Meg. It was the first really warm day of spring, and Amy, Meg, Jo, and Beth were all outdoors enjoying the sun. Meg had brought her sewing

1

with her, Jo her writing paper, and Beth one of her more damaged dolls. Amy had tried to draw them all as she saw them, except for the doll, which she gave two arms.

"It's terrible," Amy said, handing the sketch to Meg.

"No, it isn't," Meg said. "Is it, Jo?"

Amy sighed. Meg never said a cruel word to her, and Beth never said a cruel word to anybody, but Jo always took particular pleasure in making fun of Amy. Amy didn't keep her opinions of Jo to herself either, but Jo was older, and that gave her an unfair advantage, at least in Amy's eyes.

Jo looked at the sketch carefully. "It's not bad," she said. "Although you've made Beth look as though she has three eyes."

"The pencil smudged," Amy said.

"Let me see." Beth carefully put her doll down on the grass and walked over to Jo. "I think it's a lovely sketch," she said. "But why do you have Meg writing? I thought Jo was."

"That *is* Jo," Amy said. "How can you possibly mistake Meg for Jo?"

"I'm sorry," Beth said. "I think I have something in my eye."

"Which eye?" asked Jo. "Your first, second, or third?"

Meg and Beth laughed. Amy scowled.

"There, there, Amy," said Meg. "I'm sure not even Michelangelo got it right all the time."

"I never get it right," Amy said. "Never, never, never." She snatched the sheet of paper from Jo and tore it to shreds.

"I feel that way sometimes about my plays," Jo said. "They're never as good as I want them to be."

Amy was surprised. Jo wasn't one for self-criticism, especially not when it might make Amy feel better.

"I feel that way about my schoolwork," said Beth. "Amy, you're so much smarter than I am at school."

"And my sewing could be better as well," said Meg. "I see how perfectly Marmee sews and I wish I could do half as well."

"We are failures, aren't we?" Amy said, trying to take comfort from the thought.

"Not failures," said Jo. "Just not as good as we'd like to be."

"Nor should we be," said Meg. "If we were all perfect at everything, we'd have nothing to strive for."

"I'm tired of striving," Amy said. "It seems as if all we ever do is strive. Can't things just come easily for us once in a while?"

"Oh, Amy," said Beth. "Think of what Father is enduring right now, and all the brave soldiers who are fighting for the Union."

"Must I?" moaned Amy, but she immediately felt bad. Father had left two months earlier to serve as a chaplain for the Union Army. Already he had seen battle. His letters home had described the suffering of the soldiers. Amy knew that her own needs were nothing compared to theirs. "I'm sorry," she said. "I know I'm a selfish goose. But I so want to be good at my art."

"You are good," Jo said. "And you're only ten years old. You'll get better. It will just take time."

"And training," Amy said. "But how can I

5

dream of lessons when we don't even have the money for paper and pencils?"

"We're not that badly off," Meg said. "And soon Jo and I will be finished with school and will be earning money. That will help."

"You're not going to use your money to pay for my sketchpads," Amy pointed out. "It will go for food, and wood for the stove, and for things Father will need sent to him."

"Oh, dear," said Meg. "I had been hoping to use my salary for gowns and furs and diamonds."

This time Amy joined in the laughter.

"It does seem unfair," Jo said. "I'll never understand why Marmee has to scrimp and save while someone like Aunt March has all the money in Concord."

"Not all of it," Meg said. "There are plenty of wealthy families here. We've gone to school with many of them, and I've envied them their dresses and their homes."

"But Meg," Beth said. "You wouldn't trade your life for theirs, would you?"

"No," Meg said. "But I'd be happier if

they'd just share a little part of their riches with me."

"As long as it wasn't charity," Jo said. "It's bad enough when Aunt March comes calling and gives Marmee a few dollars. She acts as though we were begging on the streets and she's the only one keeping us from starvation."

"Aunt March means well," Meg said. "But she is a bit heavy-handed with her acts of kindness."

"Heavy-handed!" cried Jo. "She's as gentle as an elephant. Marmee has to endure endless sermons about how Father should have stayed home and gone into business and devoted his life to making money. As though Father or Marmee cared about such things."

The problem, as Amy saw it, was that Father and Marmee *didn't* care about such things. It would be nice, she thought, if they cared just a little more about money and a little less about doing good. Not a lot. Just a little.

"I think we'd all like it if we had more money," Meg said. "Maybe not Beth, who doesn't seem to mind. But the rest of us do,

Marmee included. I know I'd like new gloves and boots, and Jo would like to travel around the world, and Amy wants everything there is. Maybe that's wrong and selfish of us, but it's hard sometimes to see what others have and what we don't. Not that I'd change Father one bit. But I can't help wishing that he were as good-hearted and kind as he is *and* that money mattered to him a bit more."

"It wouldn't work," Jo said. "If Father had money, he'd just give it to the poor. Beth takes after him that way, don't you, Bethy?"

"I just think we have enough," Beth replied. "Although I do wish Meg could have her new boots and you your travels, Jo, and Amy everything else."

"I know you all believe I'm selfish," Amy said. "But if I were a better artist, I could make money at it. Then I'd be able to help our family the way you will be, Meg, and you too, Jo."

"Amy, you're just a child," Meg said. "No one expects you to be earning your keep."

"But when I'm older, what will become of

me?" Amy asked. "If I never get to take art lessons, I'll never be any good. Will I have to become a governess, or an old lady's companion?"

Meg and Jo were silent. Those were the very occupations they were each going to have when the school year ended.

"The war will be over soon, I'm sure of it," Beth said. "And Father will come back, and we'll have more money then. We won't be rich, but we won't be so poor either. Things will be easier."

"I won't really mind being Aunt March's companion," Jo said. "True, she's old and she's tiresome, but she has a wonderful library, and sometimes she makes me laugh."

"And I won't really mind being a governess," Meg said. "I love children. And I'll only be working until I find a man as wonderful as Father to marry and raise a family with."

"And I certainly won't mind staying home with Hannah and helping with the housework," Beth said. "I'll be glad to be away from all those other children at school."

"So it's only me?" Amy asked.

Jo laughed. "You've always been special."

"I have a thought," Meg said. "Amy, do you know Annabelle Snow? I think she has a sister in your class."

"Jenny Snow," Amy replied.

"I heard Annabelle say once that her father pays for art lessons for her and her sisters," Meg said. "Perhaps you could ask Jenny if you could share in their lessons. Annabelle is a nice girl. I'm sure she wouldn't mind."

"Art lessons," Amy said. "With a real art teacher. I'd be sure to become a great artist if I could only have art lessons."

"Then ask Jenny," Meg said, "and see if you can join her."

Art lessons from a real teacher. It was so little to ask for, Amy thought, and it held so much promise for the future.

CHAPTER 2

*A*my sat at her school desk, stared at her teacher, and willed the day to be over. It wasn't that she disliked school. Normally she enjoyed it, or at least didn't mind going. But today she eagerly awaited release from the classroom.

Quickly, she glanced at Beth, who shared the classroom with her. In just a few weeks the school year would end, and Beth would continue her studies at home. Amy loved Beth and knew she would miss her company, but Amy wasn't shy, the way Beth was, and she had many friends in class. And now there was Jenny Snow to be friends with as well.

Just thinking about Jenny, who lived in a world that Amy could only dream of—a world of art instructors and butlers and maids and grooms and gardeners and cooks and footmen—brought a smile to Amy's face. And her smile widened as even in her own greed she had to admit that she couldn't really see the need for footmen.

"Would you care to share your thoughts with us, Amy March?" Mr. Davis, Amy's teacher, asked.

But before Amy was forced to respond, the school bell rang, and she jumped up along with her classmates and raced out of the room.

"Are you going straight home?" Beth asked as they left the school building.

"Not today," Amy said. "I want to talk to Jenny Snow."

"Oh, yes," Beth said. "I hope she lets you share her art lessons."

"I hope so too," Amy said. She and Jenny had never had much to do with each other. Jenny's family was among the wealthiest in

Concord, and Jenny seemed to prefer to socialize with the other well-to-do girls. But Amy was sure that once Jenny got to know her, she'd realize Amy was every bit as much a lady, even if she didn't come from money.

"Wish me luck," Amy said. "There's Jenny now. Jenny! Oh, Jenny!"

Jenny Snow turned at the sound of her name. "Oh, it's you, Amy," she said as Amy made her way over. "What do you want?"

"I was wondering if perhaps someday you might come visit me at home," Amy replied. That had seemed the right approach the night before: extend the first invitation, and then Jenny would have to invite her in return. In fact, when Amy had imagined the conversation, Jenny had been so pleased at the invitation that she had immediately offered to include Amy in her art lessons.

"Where else might I visit you?" Jenny asked. "Do you have a summer estate you haven't told us about?"

"No, of course not," Amy said, painfully aware that the conversation was not going the way she'd imagined. "Would you like to, I mean? Visit me?"

"I suppose, if I have nothing better to do," said Jenny. "It might be fun to see those other sisters of yours again. Perhaps they've become as quiet as Beth."

"Oh, no, they haven't," Amy said. "Meg is a real lady. And Jo is full of fun." That was, Amy realized, the nicest thing she'd ever said about Jo. But it certainly was true. "Only Beth is shy. And at home she isn't nearly so bad, and she plays the piano wonderfully well."

"Do you really own a piano?" Jenny asked. "My mother says the Marches are poor as church mice. How can you afford a piano? Or was it an act of charity on the part of that rich aunt of yours?"

Amy looked at Jenny. She was a very pretty girl and always the best dressed in school. Her family had money and social position. Aunt March frequently received Jenny's parents for visits, and there was no greater social authority in Concord than Aunt March.

And Jenny was smart. She did as well in her schoolwork as Amy, and, Amy suspected, with less effort. Jenny had her choice of friends but mostly associated with Susie Perkins, a girl every bit as wealthy as she.

But Amy couldn't help wishing that Jenny Snow were a little bit nicer, the way Meg said Annabelle was. Still, no one had ever said art was easy, and if Amy had to be insulted, it was better to be insulted by someone who dressed well.

"I don't know how we got the piano," Amy responded. "We've always had it."

"We own a grand piano," Jenny said. "It has a place of honor in our music room. A piano tuner from Boston comes twice a year to tune it. Papa loves good music, and Mama plays like an angel. Both of them have encouraged my sisters and me to appreciate fine music. And so we take piano lessons with a music teacher who comes once a week. Papa and Mama also believe that a lady should be able to sing all the finest songs. For that we have a singing teacher come once a month to teach us

15

the very newest. And of course art lessons are important as well."

"Of course they are," Amy said, delighted that Jenny had brought the subject up. "Do you know that I draw?"

"Everyone knows," said Jenny. "There isn't a soul in Concord you haven't told. And I suppose you are a good little artist, for someone with no training. But my sisters and I receive weekly art lessons, and so we've learned the really best way of sketching."

"I should love that," Amy said. "An art instructor."

"I prefer the dancing master," Jenny declared. "He works with my sisters and me on the formal dances we shall need to know when the time comes to make our debuts. Mama says a truly well-bred lady needs art as well as music and dancing, and that is why we employ an art instructor."

"I want to be an artist," Amy said. "I want to paint beautiful works in oils."

"I suppose that's as respectable a job as any," said Jenny. "Of course, my sisters and I will never have to earn our livelihood." She laughed. "Mama and Papa would have fits if they even *thought* that might happen. No, we'll make the very best sorts of marriages, and live in the finest homes, and see to it that our daughters have music lessons and art lessons and dancing lessons just as we did, so that they too can make the best sorts of marriages."

That seemed like a terrible waste of art lessons to Amy. But if the lessons were so unimportant to Jenny and her sisters, Amy felt it was all the more reason why Jenny should be willing to have her share them. "How wonderful that all sounds," she said. "But would you like to visit me?"

"I suppose I should sometime," Jenny replied. "My mother says that while your family has no money at all, you do have breeding, and we should never look down on those who are as good as we are simply because they've fallen on hard times."

"How kind of her," said Amy.

Jenny gave Amy a searching look, and then she smiled. "Mama does go on sometimes,"

17

she said. "And I suspect I do myself. But Concord is so boring compared to New York and London. Even Boston. And Mama frets that the very best sort of husband simply won't appear here, and so we're being trained to compete against the belles of New York and London and Boston. It is so important to make the right marriage, you know. Your entire happiness depends upon it."

Amy thought of Marmee and Father. They had very little money, but they certainly had made the right marriage. "Your mother is right," she said. "I hope someday I'll make the right marriage also."

"Perhaps you will," Jenny said, but before Amy had a chance to set a date for Jenny to visit her, Jenny walked over to Susie Perkins.

Amy sighed. She knew Marmee was a lady every bit as fine as Jenny's mother must be. What a crime it was that the Marches didn't have any money! And what a shame that Amy was no closer to art lessons than she had been the day before.

CHAPTER 3

"*L*ook at her."
"Have you ever seen a more beautiful girl?"
"What a beautiful dress."
"Who is she, do you know?"

Amy was aware of all the whispers as she and Beth walked through the school yard the next day. Someday she hoped to elicit similar whispers about herself.

But for now all the attention was being paid to a new girl. Beth caught sight of her first, and even she was impressed. "Look at her, Amy," she whispered. "She's beside the door."

Amy finally saw the girl the others were speaking of. And she was beautiful, with raven-black hair and the face of an angel. Her dress was quite the loveliest Amy had ever seen, even finer than any Jenny Snow wore. But the new girl didn't seem to have any airs about her. In fact, she seemed almost nervous standing by herself.

"Poor girl," said Beth. "It's so hard to be shy."

Amy couldn't believe that any girl that pretty could be shy. "She's just new, that's all," she said. "I'll prove it to you." And she made her way to the school door with Beth trailing behind.

"Good morning," Amy said. "Are you new here? I'd be happy to help you if you are."

The beautiful girl smiled at Amy and became, if that was possible, even lovelier. "My family just moved to Concord," she said. "Papa thought it would be best for me to attend school right away and not wait until the next year begins. My name is Diana Hughes, and I'll be in Mr. Davis's class."

"We're in that class as well," Amy said. "I'm Amy March, and this is my sister Beth."

Diana's face lit with joy. "Are you really Amy March?" she asked. "And are you really Beth? And do you have two other sisters and a father who has just joined the Union Army as a chaplain?"

"We have," Amy said.

"Why, this is so splendid," Diana said. "My father went to school with your father. It was his hope to see him when we moved here, but we heard that your father had already left for his noble work. My father paid a call on your great-aunt, Mrs. March, you see, and she told him of you and your sisters. I was so hoping to meet you. Now I don't feel nearly so alone."

"It is difficult to be the new girl," Amy said, although she had never been the new girl in her life. "If there's anything my sisters or I can do for you, don't hesitate to ask."

"Might I have lunch with you both?" Diana asked. "I've been dreading eating alone."

"But of course. We insist you join us," Amy said. "Don't we, Beth?"

"It would be very nice if you did," Beth said. "Why don't you come with us now? We can show you the classroom."

"Thank you," Diana said. "Wait until I tell Papa that the nicest girls in my new school turned out to be Amy and Beth March."

A seat was found for Diana, and once classes commenced, Amy noticed that the other girls were inspecting Diana. One or two of them, she saw, looked first at Diana and then at Amy, as though trying to determine why the girls had become such fast friends. Amy loved the attention.

The looks and whispers continued even as lunchtime arrived and everyone went outdoors to eat in the warm weather. Amy saw to it that she and Diana claimed a comfortable spot under a budding oak tree. Beth joined them, but it was Diana whom Amy sat next to.

"Our cook prepared such a feast for me," Diana said. "I told her there would be far too much for me to eat, but she simply couldn't be stopped. You and Beth will help me, won't you, by sharing with me?"

"If you insist," said Amy, looking at Diana's lunch. It was indeed a feast, especially compared to what Hannah, the Marches' housekeeper, had packed for her and Beth.

"But you must have some of ours as well," Beth said. "Hannah makes us wonderful turnovers. We each have one every day for lunch. Please take mine, Diana."

"They look delicious," Diana said. "But I couldn't possibly eat an entire one and do justice to my own lunch. Here, I'll take half, and give you half of mine." The half she handed to Beth was enough food to feed Beth and her sisters an entire meal.

"Amy, help me," Beth pleaded, and Amy cheerfully took some of the bounty from her older sister.

The girls sat under the tree, making, Amy knew, a lovely picture. Much to her delight, Jenny Snow and Susie Perkins soon walked over to them.

"Hello," Jenny said, addressing Diana. "We saw you were new here and wondered if you needed any help."

23

"How kind of you," Diana said with a lovely smile. "I'm fine right now, as you can see. I'm sharing lunch with Amy and Beth March. You should taste their turnovers. They're even better than what my cook prepared for me."

"We saw you were having lunch with Amy and Beth," Susie Perkins said. "Are you acquainted with the Marches?"

"Our families have known each other for years," Diana said. "My father has always repeated that there is no man better in this world than Mr. March. And his daughters are true reflections of him, for when they saw I was alone this morning, they came to my assistance right away. And that before we even realized that our fathers shared such a strong connection."

Jenny and Susie sat down by Diana, ever so slightly brushing Amy and Beth aside as they did. "We all love the March girls," Jenny said. "Amy is so clever and Beth so sweet and shy. And their father is the noblest of creatures. But it wouldn't do for you to spend all your time with them alone."

"And why not?" asked Amy.

"Because that would be selfish of you," said Susie. "Diana should get to know all the best girls in our class. How else will she see who she would most enjoy being friends with?"

"She's been here only four hours," Amy said sharply.

"My mama says one can always tell true breeding immediately," declared Jenny. "I knew from the moment I saw you that you were as fine a girl as there is in Concord, Diana. Tell us, where did you come from before moving here?"

"We lived in Philadelphia," Diana said. "But Papa thought it would be best if we were raised here, now that my mother is no longer with us."

"You poor child, to be motherless," said Susie. "Have you brothers and sisters to share in your grief?"

"A brother," said Diana. "Older than I am. He'll finish the school year here and then go away to continue his studies. But Papa believes the schools in Concord are excellent and will provide me with the education I need."

"My father feels just the same way," said Jenny. "Although, of course, when the time comes, I'll be sent to finishing school for a year or two."

Diana nodded. "Papa says I should finish my education with a year in Switzerland. But not before I'm sixteen."

"Switzerland," said Susie. "Just the place."

"I do love it there," Diana said. "Although Paris is much livelier."

"Have you spent much time there?" asked Jenny.

"We've traveled abroad a great deal," Diana replied. "Tell me, Amy, have you been abroad?"

Jenny laughed before Amy even had a chance to speak. "The Marches travel?" she asked. "Oh, I'm sorry. Beth went to New York once—didn't she?—for a week. And she came back having met a very famous person."

"She met Abraham Lincoln," Amy said. "Didn't you, Beth?"

But Beth didn't answer. Amy noticed that she had moved ever so slightly away, until it almost appeared that she was no longer part of their group.

"Someday I'll travel," Amy said. "I want to study art in Europe. I don't suppose you have an art instructor, Diana."

Diana was silent for a moment. "No," she said. "Father doesn't care for private instruction."

"Oh," Amy said with disappointment. Now she still had to hope that Jenny Snow would offer to share her art lessons.

Nothing, Amy thought with a sigh, ever came easily for the Marches.

CHAPTER 4

As lunch began the next day, Jenny walked at Diana's right side, and Susie on Diana's left. Amy found herself a step or two behind, and Beth, she noticed, didn't bother to keep up at all.

The girls sat under the same tree Amy had picked for them the day before, but now Amy was crowded out, and even without Beth there, she found herself half under the tree and half in the bright May sun.

"It is so hot for this time of year," Jenny said languidly as she hid under the shade of the tree.

"Poor Amy will freckle and blister," said Susie, not offering to give up her shady spot. "She'll look a sight tomorrow, I'm sure."

"Amy, take my place," Diana offered.

"Oh, no, don't do that," said Susie. "You mustn't risk darkening your beautiful skin, Diana."

"I'm sure that's no worse than freckles and blisters," Diana declared. "Amy, come here, and sit between Jenny and Susie."

"If you like," said Amy, delighted at the chance. But when Diana got up to change places, the other girls moved slightly, so that there was room for all four of them under the tree.

"This is so cozy," said Susie, looking on with annoyance as Amy spread her skirt out a bit. "Amy March!" she cried. "Don't be such a hog."

"I'm sorry," said Amy, and moved an inch closer to Jenny.

"I'm sorry Beth hasn't joined us," Diana said. "Susie, you're nearest to her. Why don't you invite her over?"

"There's hardly space for the four of us," said Susie. "Let alone another March girl."

"Beth is terribly shy," said Jenny. "We all make allowances for it. She and Amy frequently eat lunch by themselves. Don't you, Amy?"

Amy was uncertain how to answer. While it was true that on many occasions she ate with Beth, there were just as many times when she ate with friends and Beth either joined them or ate alone. When Jo had attended the school, there had been no problem, for Beth had eaten with her. But as much as Amy loved Beth, she didn't want to give up all her friendships just to keep her quiet sister company.

"Beth seems such a dear," said Diana. "I do look forward to meeting your other sisters, Amy, and getting to know them as well."

"Meg March is quite nice," said Jenny. "My sister, Annabelle, knows her very well. Everyone agrees it's a shame she has no money, for she really is respectable. But Jo is a terror! In many ways, Amy is the best of the March sisters."

31

Amy was startled to hear Jenny speak so highly of her. Of course anyone would come off well compared to Jo.

"I hope I'll be asked soon to pay a call on all the March sisters," Diana said. "And their mother."

"Amy invited me for a visit just the other day," said Jenny. "Of course, with all the lessons I take, piano and art and dancing, it's terribly hard for me to fit another engagement into my social calendar."

"How unfortunate," said Diana. "For I was thinking of asking you to my house. But now I see you wouldn't have the time, so I'll spare myself the disappointment and not ask."

"Oh, no," said Jenny. "That is to say, of course I could find the time should you ask."

Diana smiled. "First I must ask Amy," she said. "For she was my first friend in Concord. Amy, you will come visit me, won't you? I should dearly love for you to meet my brother and my father."

"I'd be glad to," Amy said, wishing that

Jenny had been the one to invite her. Still, if Amy met Diana's father, perhaps she could convince him of the value of private art lessons for Diana and her friends.

Diana clapped her hands in delight. "This Saturday?" she asked. "And I should so like it if Beth would join us. Do ask her, Amy. What pleasure it would bring me to have you both there!"

"And after Amy visits, you'll be sure to ask me," Jenny said. "I understand social obligations." She leaned closer to Diana and lowered her voice to a near whisper. "I'm sure you feel you must ask Amy first, since your father knows hers, but once you've done your part, you can invite the girls you truly wish to be friends with."

Amy heard every word, and though her face grew hot with anger, she didn't say a thing.

"I am very blessed, then," Diana said loudly. "Since it is Amy and Beth I want to be friends with."

"Once you get to know me, I'm sure you'll

value my friendship as well," Jenny said. "Won't she, Amy?"

"My friendship also," Susie said. "Won't she, Amy?"

Amy's anger vanished and she tried hard not to laugh. "Jenny and Susie have much to offer," she said.

"I don't know how Papa will feel if I invite too many girls to visit," Diana replied. "I know he'll approve of Beth and Amy. But he might not permit me other callers."

"I'm sure he will when you tell him that my family is one of the finest in all of Massachusetts," Jenny said.

"Mine is as well," said Susie.

Diana smiled at them. "How wonderful for you that you have each other," she said. "Amy, do tell me more about your sisters. Is Meg as lovely as I hear? And Jo must be quite extraordinary, the way people talk of her."

Just then the school bell rang, calling the girls to return to their classes. Amy rose, and Diana stood as well, once again extending the invitation for Amy and Beth to visit on Saturday.

Amy gladly accepted for herself, saying she would be sure to let Beth know. She was pleased that Jenny and Susie were listening. It had become obvious to her during lunch that Jenny would never care for her friendship, but perhaps if Diana and Amy became friends, Jenny might at least tolerate Amy so that she could have a chance at Diana. And that would open the door for Amy to share in Jenny's art lessons.

Amy could hear the voices of her family inside her. Marmee instructed her that it was wrong to use one girl to make friends with another. Jo made nasty comments about Jenny and her snobbishness. Even Meg, who understood Amy better than anybody else, seemed to say that Diana was a hundred times nicer than Jenny and that Amy should be pleased with her offer of friendship and should not use her for personal gain.

But none of the voices was real, and Amy

was much relieved. If Diana wanted to be friends, that was fine, and Amy would be nice to her. But it was what Jenny had to offer that Amy truly wanted, and if Diana was a means to that end, then so be it.

CHAPTER 5

As Amy and Beth approached their house that afternoon, they saw Aunt March's carriage parked in the road. "Oh, no," Beth said. "Aunt March. Where can we hide?"

"Aunt March isn't so bad," Amy said. She was actually rather fond of their great-aunt.

"I'm glad you think so," Beth said. "But she scares me. Even when she's being nice, she makes me nervous."

"Then go visit Mr. Emerson," Amy suggested. "He's said we're welcome to call on him any time we want. And I'm sure you want to now."

Beth looked relieved. "What a good idea. I haven't seen nearly as much of him since Father left. I'll call on him right away and tell him how Father is doing."

"He'll be glad to hear," Amy said. "Go now, before Aunt March realizes we've returned."

Beth smiled gratefully at Amy. Amy smiled back, and Beth ran down the road. Amy was glad she didn't suffer from shyness the way Beth did. It must be awful to be frightened of the world.

"I'm home, Marmee," Amy said as she entered the house.

"We're in the parlor," Marmee replied.

Amy joined her mother and great-aunt. Amy kissed Marmee first, then gave Aunt March a peck on the cheek. Aunt March expected that and no more, and Amy was happy to oblige.

"How was your school day?" Marmee asked. "And where's Bethy?"

"She decided to pay a call on Mr. Emerson," Amy said. "She sends her apologies, Aunt March."

Aunt March *humph*ed. "I think that child expects I'll eat her," she said.

"Bethy's that way with everyone," Marmee said. "But she cherishes her friendship with Mr. Emerson."

"I'm glad Amy has deigned to join us," Aunt March said. "Actually, it's you I wished to speak to."

"Me?" Amy asked. Aunt March was capable of unexpected acts of generosity. Perhaps someone, Jo even, had suggested private art instructions for Amy.

"I believe a new girl has entered your school," Aunt March said instead. "Diana Hughes."

"Oh, yes," Amy said. "Diana mentioned that her father had called on you."

"That he did," Aunt March said. "The Hugheses have always been a most respectable family. John Hughes attended school with your father, Amy."

Amy nodded. "Diana told me that. She seems very nice."

"I'm sure she is a good girl," Aunt March said. "Her family has endured great suffering of late."

Amy tried to see how any girl as wealthy and pretty as Diana could suffer, but then she remembered Diana's mentioning that her mother was no longer with them. Amy couldn't imagine life without Marmee, and her heart went out to Diana and her father for their loss.

"Do you like Diana?" Marmee asked.

"Oh, yes," Amy replied. "She's very pleasant. Beth and I were the first girls to greet her when she started school. She was so glad to learn who we were that she's offered us her friendship ever since."

Aunt March pursed her lips. "It may be hard for Diana to make friendships with the other girls," she said. "But I trust you will do your duty, Amy."

"Diana invited me to her house on Saturday," Amy said. "She did say something about her father not wanting her to have too many callers, but she was sure I'd be welcome because of Father."

"It must be difficult for Mr. Hughes," Marmee said.

"Very difficult," Aunt March agreed. "But the situation is hardly of his making. Still, it's hard to know what will become of his daughter."

"We must all be very kind to her," Marmee murmured. She reached out to Amy and patted her head. "I know I can count on you, Amy, to treat Diana with the utmost kindness."

"Of course, Marmee," Amy said. She sensed that Marmee and Aunt March were keeping something from her. But it didn't matter. It would be easy enough for her to be nice to Diana.

"You're a good girl, Amy," Aunt March said. "You've done your duty to your great-aunt. You may go outside now and join your sisters. I believe they're hiding in the bushes somewhere."

"Aunt March!" Marmee said, but the old woman just shook her head.

"Good-bye, Aunt March," Amy said. She left the house by way of the kitchen, taking a carrot from Hannah as she went. Sure enough, Meg and Jo were outside, sitting under the apple tree, which was just beginning to bloom.

"Aunt March says you're hiding from her," Amy told them, then took a bite of her carrot.

"We've already paid our respects," Meg said. "And it's such a beautiful day, we couldn't bear to stay inside."

"And Beth managed to get away," Jo said. "We saw her heading toward Mr. Emerson's house. I wish I'd thought of that."

"Did Aunt March mention anything about Diana Hughes to you?" Amy asked as she made herself comfortable under the apple tree.

Jo shook her head. "She merely told me to dress more neatly and to stand up straighter," she said. "The usual comments. Meg, did she say anything to you?"

"No," Meg said. "But I did get the feeling

we'd interrupted something. Diana's the new girl in your class, isn't she?"

Amy nodded. "Aunt March said I should be kind to her," she said. "Diana certainly is the prettiest girl I've ever seen, and she dresses beautifully. Her father must be quite wealthy. Jenny Snow and Susie Perkins already want to be her friends, but Diana seems to prefer my company."

"She doesn't sound like someone who needs your kindness," Jo said.

"Aunt March mentioned a 'situation,'" Amy said. "Are you sure you don't know what it could be?"

"All I know is that when we entered the house Marmee and Aunt March stopped talking," Meg said. "Aunt March whispered about little pitchers with big ears."

"So she did," Jo said. "I just assumed she meant my ears were too big. Aunt March is always looking for new things to criticize me about."

"Your ears haven't grown since the last time she saw you," Meg said. "I imagine there's something about Diana that Aunt March doesn't care for us to know."

"I haven't got a clue what it could be," Amy said.

"If Diana wants you to know, she'll tell you herself," Jo said. "We shouldn't be sitting here trying to guess other people's private affairs."

"Still, it would be interesting to learn more," Meg said.

"I'll be visiting Diana on Saturday," Amy said. "If I find out anything, I'll be sure to tell you."

"Don't be a little snoop," Jo said.

"Amy won't be," Meg said. "But it would be fun to learn something that Aunt March doesn't want us to know!"

CHAPTER 6

*I*t was a long walk from the Marches' home
to where Diana lived, and Amy hoped the
Hugheses had a carriage she could ride
home in after her visit. The weather was perfect for walking, but a carriage ride would be a
particular treat over such a long distance.

Beth had chosen not to come with her, and
Amy was glad. She hoped once word spread
that she'd been Diana's only guest, Jenny
Snow would start thinking of her as someone
special—as someone worthy of her own
friendship. And without Beth there, it might
be easier to find out what Aunt March had
been talking about with Marmee.

As Amy approached Diana's home, she wondered, not for the first time, why Diana liked her so much, and why she seemed so reluctant to make other friends. It had been Amy's experience that the rich girls in Concord tended to be friends with the other rich girls. True, Meg and Amy both had been friends with girls far wealthier than they, but that was because the Marches were a well-respected family, even if their income was limited.

Diana certainly knew that about the Marches, but Amy still would have expected Diana to favor Jenny and Susie, who dressed almost as well as Diana and were just as likely to finish their education in Switzerland.

Whatever the reason, Amy couldn't help feeling pleased that she was paying a call on such a fine family. She was especially pleased when she rang the doorbell and the door was opened by a butler. Amy thoroughly approved of households with butlers.

The butler informed Diana of Amy's arrival, and Diana soon joined Amy in the front parlor.

"What a splendid home," Amy said. Diana's family seemed to own even more things than Aunt March, and their taste was every bit as good.

"Father likes to collect antiques," Diana said.

"So does Aunt March," Amy said. "Although Jo says she's a bit of an antique herself!"

Diana looked taken aback, but then she smiled. "Mrs. March has many beautiful things in her home," she said. "Father admired a silver Revere bowl in particular."

Amy took a step toward a painting on the wall. It was a portrait of a man whose expression was as somber as the dark gray and brown painted colors. Amy wasn't sure whether she liked it or not.

"That's a Rembrandt self-portrait," Diana said. "It's the pride of Father's collection. You have a wonderful eye, Amy, to have gone to it first."

Amy was reluctant to admit she didn't know how she felt about the painting. "It has a place

47

of honor," she pointed out. "I was bound to notice it right away."

"That's what I like about you, Amy," said Diana. "You're honest and quite modest."

No one had ever called Amy modest before. She smiled when she thought of what Jo would have said if she'd heard Diana's comment.

"You're lucky to live in such a grand house," Amy said, her eyes taking in all the wonders Mr. Hughes had collected. "There are so many beautiful things here. I'd love to sketch them."

"Then you must visit me often," Diana said. "And bring your sketchbook so that you can draw the things you like best."

"Thank you," Amy said with a smile. "I should like that."

"I'm so glad," Diana said. "Let me show you the rest of the house. We have a lovely painting in the dining room and another fine one in the back parlor. Those are Father's favorites, so I suppose they must be the best."

Amy followed Diana on the tour of the house. Diana paused in front of every item Amy found particularly striking and described its background. Most of the artwork had been purchased on family trips to Europe.

"You're so fortunate to be able to travel," Amy said. "I long to see the world."

Diana laughed. "And I envy girls who stay in one place for a year at a time," she said. "Father collects and collects, but he's never satisfied and always goes off to collect some more. I know I should be grateful that he takes my brother, David, and me with him, but David spends most of his time with his tutor and I with my governess, so we don't see much of Father anyway. I'd be happiest if I could attend the same school year after year. Traveling can be terribly lonely."

"It must be hard," Amy said. "I'm never lonely."

"How could you be?" said Diana. "You have many friends at school. And of course, you always have your sisters for company."

"My sisters are my dearest friends," Amy said. "I can't imagine what life would be like without them."

"I do look forward to meeting Meg and Jo," Diana said. "Do you think they'll like me?"

"How could they not?" replied Amy. "I've already told them how nice you are. Now show me your room, and let me see your personal treasures."

Diana took Amy by the hand and led her upstairs. "This is my sanctuary," she said. "Do you like it?"

Amy loved it. Her own room, which she shared with Beth, was filled with Beth's ragtag collection of dolls and her own sketches and art supplies. There was scarcely enough space for their beds.

But Diana's room was four times as large, and while it was filled with dolls and books and games, there was ample space for a bed with a canopy, two large chairs, and an armoire that Amy just knew was filled with beautiful dresses.

"This is the most wonderful room I've ever seen," she said quite honestly. "I wish mine were a tenth as nice."

"Father denies me nothing," Diana said. "If he sees something he thinks I might like, a doll or a book, he purchases it for me. I suppose I'm rather spoiled."

"You don't seem spoiled," Amy said. It occurred to her that Mr. Hughes would be happy to give his daughter art lessons if she wanted them. All that was needed was a little push, and Amy was more than willing to provide that. "I know my father would give us all we wanted if he could afford to. Especially if he thought it would improve us."

"I'm sure he would," Diana replied. "Father says ministers do God's work and that is far more worthy than commerce. But commerce does pay more."

"Beth would love your dolls," Amy said, picking one up and looking at it carefully. It had a lovely bisque head, and the lace on its pantaloons appeared to be French.

"Then I must give you one to take to her," Diana said. "Do you think she would like the one you're holding?"

"Oh, no," Amy said putting the doll down quickly. "That isn't necessary."

"I have so many dolls I can hardly remember what they look like," Diana said. "And Father certainly wouldn't mind. How about this one? Do you think Beth would like it?" She handed Amy a magnificent china doll that wore a silk dress.

"You should give it to Beth yourself," Amy said. "It would mean more to her that way."

"Then I'll give you something instead," Diana said. "How about this necklace? You have an eye for pretty things, and it would look so nice on you, Amy. Please take it."

Amy held the necklace Diana offered her. On the beautiful gold chain hung an even more beautiful oval gold locket.

"No, thank you," Amy said, handing the necklace back. "I could never repay you."

"But you've offered me your friendship, and that's worth a hundred necklaces," Diana said.

"Please, won't you take it as a token of my gratitude?"

Amy stared wistfully at the necklace. There was no point in accepting it, since Marmee would insist she return it. "You have nothing to be grateful for," she said. "I'm sure you'll make many more friends during your stay in Concord."

"It's so easy for you," Diana said. "I wish it were for me."

Amy longed to ask Diana what the situation was that had made Aunt March whisper about her. But she feared that bringing it up might upset Diana. "Is your father home?" she asked instead. "Or your brother? I would like to meet them."

"My brother is in his room," Diana said. "Father is out, but he's hoping to return before you leave. Come, meet David. An older brother is the one treasure I have that you don't."

"It must be nice to have an older brother," Amy said as she and Diana headed down the hallway.

"It is," Diana said. "David and I are very close. I hate to think what life will be like next year when he goes off to school. I'll be even lonelier than before."

"I'll be here," Amy said. "I know it's not the same, but we'll do things together and that will help." She pictured herself with Diana, the two of them taking art lessons together. It was pleasant not to have to include Jenny in the fantasy.

"That would be nice," Diana said. "I'm so glad you're here." She gave Amy a quick kiss on the cheek, then knocked on the door in front of them. A boy's voice told them to enter.

"Amy, I'd like you to meet my brother, David," Diana said. "David, this is Amy March, my friend from school."

"Hello, Amy," David said. He was seated at his desk, but rose as Diana made her introductions. He seemed to be two or three years older than Diana, and while Diana had dark hair and remarkable violet eyes, David's hair was light brown and his eyes were hazel. "My sister has told me a great deal about you, how kind you and your sister have been to befriend her."

"It's easy to be friends with Diana," Amy said. "Everybody likes her at school."

"I'm glad," David said with a grin. "We like her a great deal ourselves."

Amy laughed. David was obviously a warm and funny older brother. Briefly she wondered which of her sisters she'd be willing to trade for such a brother. Diana was so friendly, she might even go along with the idea. The thought brought a smile to Amy's face.

Diana laughed also. "It's good to hear you laugh," David said. "You don't laugh enough these days, Diana."

"Having Amy here makes me happy," Diana said.

"Then she must come more often," David declared. "You will, won't you, Amy? I know Father would be pleased if you did. He speaks so highly of your family."

"My great-aunt March feels the same about yours," Amy said. "She said your father is highly respectable."

The smiles faded from David and Diana's faces. "It's good to know she feels that way," David said. "Respectability can't be over-rated—especially as it's so easy to lose."

"David," Diana said. "Don't be harsh."

"I mean it," David said. "It's always good when a lady such as Mrs. March bestows her approval on us."

"Did I say something wrong?" Amy asked.

"No, of course not." Diana sounded suddenly stiff. "David, what were you working on when we came in?"

"History," he replied. "Never my favorite subject. It makes me think about the past too much."

"Art is what I like best," Amy said. This seemed as good a time as any to broach the subject. "Of course, we don't receive art lessons at school."

"I'm sure there are plenty of other things for you to learn," David said. "Reading and arithmetic and history and all that."

"Oh, yes," Amy agreed. "The school day is

always very busy. But some families think it's a good idea for their children, their daughters in particular, to have additional instruction at home. Art lessons in particular. They're all the rage."

"Are they?" David asked. "Not in this home, I suspect."

"I told you, Amy," Diana said. "Father doesn't approve of private lessons."

"But they can be so beneficial," Amy said. "All the best families offer them to their children. The best families with money, that is."

"Amy, please, Father isn't keen on discussing the subject," Diana said. "He feels we'll do just as well without—"

"You're a fool, Diana," David interrupted. "Can't you see why Amy is so insistent?" He no longer looked like the friendly boy Amy had met only moments before. "I don't know what your great-aunt told you when she mentioned how respectable we all are," he said, now looking straight at Amy. "Perhaps she only hinted at the scandal, or perhaps she sim-

ply came right out and declared that Mother is a fallen woman."

"David!" Diana pleaded.

"That's what she is, and we both know it," David shouted. "It's safe to assume your friend here knows it as well. Do you want all the details, Amy? Or did Mrs. March tell you about the riding instructor as well?"

Amy turned pale. "Aunt March said nothing. I swear it. I simply thought art lessons were a good idea."

"You see!" Diana cried. "Now Amy knows our secret when she didn't before. David, how could you?"

"Diana, I'm sorry," David said. "I just assumed from what Amy was saying that her aunt had told her the whole miserable story."

"Thanks to you, I've lost the only friend I could have in this town!" Diana cried. "I'll never speak to you again, David. Never!" She ran out of David's room and into her own. Amy heard her slam the door.

"I'm sorry," David said, and he looked close to tears himself.

"It's all right. I'll see myself out." Amy left the room and walked down the great staircase. This time she was just as happy not to see the butler. She opened the front door for herself and began the long walk home.

CHAPTER 7

"*D*id you have a good time at Diana's?" Meg asked Amy after her return. "Was her home filled with splendors?"

"More than you can imagine," Amy replied. She was seated in Meg and Jo's room. Both her sisters were sitting on their beds, and Beth now joined them. "Diana offered me a doll for Beth and a gold locket necklace for myself, but I said no to both presents."

"She sounds like a very generous girl," Meg said.

"You did the right thing to say no," Jo declared. "I'm proud of you, Amy. I know how much you like pretty things."

Ordinarily Amy enjoyed praise, and Jo was usually slow to offer it to her. But Amy's mind was on other matters.

"Did you meet Diana's family?" Meg asked.

"Just David, her brother," Amy replied. "Her father was out."

"What's her brother like?" Beth asked. "Is he as nice as Diana?"

"He seemed nice at first," Amy replied.

"At first?" Jo asked. "Amy, did you provoke him in any way?"

"No," Amy said. "At least, I didn't mean to."

"Oh, Amy," Jo said. "You insisted on snooping, didn't you? And you didn't even do a good job of it."

"I did not," Amy said. "It wasn't my fault. David simply assumed I knew things that I didn't."

"What sorts of things?" Jo asked.

"I'm not sure," Amy admitted. "But it got him very upset."

"Was Diana upset too?" Beth asked.

"Yes, she was," Amy said. "Even more than David."

"What exactly did you say?" Jo asked.

"Nothing," Amy insisted. "Nothing. I just mentioned that some girls are given art lessons at home. Is there anything wrong with that? Well, is there, Jo?"

"I suppose not," Jo said. "But you say it disturbed Diana and her brother?"

Amy nodded.

"Do you know why?" Meg asked.

Amy took a deep breath. "I think so. But I'm not completely sure. Meg, what's a fallen woman?"

"A fallen woman?" Meg repeated. "Did David or Diana use that phrase?"

"David did," Amy said.

Jo and Meg exchanged glances. "Perhaps you should ask Marmee," Meg said.

"I don't think she'd want me to ask her," Amy said. "And don't tell me to ask Aunt March. I don't want to learn about it from her."

"A fallen woman is one who has sinned," Beth said. "Isn't that right, Meg?"

"And how would you know about fallen women?" Jo asked. "Who's been filling your ears with lurid tales?"

"You have," Beth said. "It was in one of your plays. *The Ruin of the Rodolfos*, I think. One of your characters was a fallen woman, and I remember Father saying to Marmee that he wasn't sure it was a good idea for Meg to be playing that part."

"I'd forgotten all about it," Jo said. "*The Ruin of the Rodolfos* wasn't one of my best efforts. But you're right, it did have a fallen woman, and now that you mention it, Father did suggest that I change it to a woman falsely accused. Do you remember that part, Meg?"

Meg shook her head. "There have been so many parts. I don't recall that one clearly."

"I don't understand," Amy said. "We all sin."

"Speak for yourself," Jo said. "I personally am sinless."

"I didn't realize anger and impatience were virtues," Meg said with a laugh. "Sisters, we have a saint in our midst."

"Does that make Jo a fallen woman?" Amy asked. "Because she has a bad temper?"

Meg and Jo laughed even louder. "There are sins," Jo said, "and there are sins."

"Doesn't being a fallen woman have to do with babies?" Beth asked. "I'm sure I remember Father and Marmee discussing such a woman once, and she had had a baby."

"Aunt March is right," Jo said. "Little pitchers do have big ears. No wonder you keep so quiet all the time, Bethy. It gives you an opportunity to overhear the most interesting conversations."

Amy looked at Beth with greater respect. Maybe that *was* a reason Beth was so quiet. Amy frequently felt as though she missed things of great importance because she was extremely sociable and didn't listen enough.

"Do all fallen women have babies?" Amy

asked. "Or is the only way you can have a baby to be a fallen woman?"

Meg and Jo shrieked with laughter. "Really, Meg," Jo said between her howls. "We must correct this poor child's peculiar notions."

"Very well," Meg said, trying to control her laughter. "Amy, you know that men and women marry so that they can have children and become a family, as Father and Marmee have."

"Of course I know that," Amy said. "I'm not a baby."

"No, you're not," Meg said. "If you were, you wouldn't be asking about fallen women. Very well. There are some men, cads and bounders, who prey on women and take advantage of their desire to marry and become mothers."

"They're bad men," Beth said.

"The very worst," Meg agreed. "Before Father left, he had a long talk with Jo and me and warned us about such men. He said we must always be careful that the men we give our hearts to are worthy of our affections."

"Would they make you fallen women?" Amy asked. "Is that what cads and bounders do?"

"That is exactly what they do," Jo said. "They toy with the affections of girls and leave them with their reputations destroyed."

"Then it's never a woman's fault," Amy said. "A bad man turns her into a fallen woman."

"I think it's a bit more complicated than that," Meg tried to explain. "A woman can lead a man into sin, after all."

Amy sighed. "This is so confusing. If a woman is married and has children, how can she fall?"

"She can leave her husband for another man," Meg replied. "And that is the worst sin a woman can commit, because she betrays the trust of her husband and her children."

"And what becomes of her?" Amy asked. "Once she is a fallen woman?"

"Society shuns her," Meg said. "An inno-

cent girl who falls victim to a cad can be for-
given. But a married woman who leaves her
husband to take up with another man never
can be."

"Father and Marmee would forgive her,"
Beth said. "They say one must always have
one's heart open to a sinner if one wants to
lead him back to the path of righteousness."

"Father is a minister," Meg pointed out.
"And Marmee's heart is pure gold. But someone like Aunt March would never accept a
fallen woman."

"What about her family?" Amy asked.
"How should they be treated?"

"They haven't done anything wrong," Beth
said. "Why should people treat them badly?"

"I don't know," Jo said. "But sometimes
they do. Don't they, Meg? Aunt March told
me once of a girl from a fine family in Boston
whose mother ran off with the music teacher.
The girl's chances at a good marriage were
ruined."

"It doesn't have to be a music teacher, does

it?" Amy asked, thinking of David's reference to the riding instructor.

"No, of course not," Meg said. "Why? Did Mrs. Hughes really run off with a man? Do you know what sort he was?"

"Really Meg," Jo said. "I'm curious too, but we shouldn't prod Amy for the nasty details."

"I suppose not," Meg said with a sigh. "What were we talking about?"

"What happens to a girl if her mother becomes a fallen woman," Amy said. "What Aunt March told you."

"Yes, that's right," Meg said. "Aunt March's point was that the shame of one member of a family can reflect upon the whole family. I'm fairly sure she told Jo that story to warn her to behave herself. I doubt she thought Marmee was about to run off with anybody."

"I don't plan to either," Jo said. "And if I were going to lead a life of sin, it wouldn't be with a music teacher."

"It's really nothing to joke about," Meg said.

"A family such as ours has no money. All we have is our respectability, which comes from leading lives of high moral purpose. But our standing in the community is far higher than that of a woman who has betrayed her husband."

"I still think we should forgive," Beth said. "Who are we to cast the first stone?"

"We're not casting any stones," Jo said. "But I can't speak for the rest of Concord."

"Jo's right," Meg said. "I don't know exactly what David and Diana told you, Amy. And I respect the fact that you're not telling us more, much as I want to hear it. But you must keep absolutely quiet about this with everyone else."

"You really must," Jo said. "Diana's life could be a misery if everyone finds out her mother has sinned. And she doesn't sound like someone who deserves that."

"She isn't," Amy said.

"I won't say anything," Beth promised.

"None of us will," Jo said. "Will we, Amy?"

"Do be discreet," Meg said. "You could see

how curious I was, and I don't even know Diana."

Amy nodded. By that point, she would have been just as happy not to know Diana herself.

CHAPTER 8

*D*iana wasn't at school on Monday, and Amy was relieved not to see her. Amy was uncertain how to behave with Diana now that she knew just what her mother had done to become a fallen woman.

"Do you want to have lunch outside?" Amy asked Beth when the bell rang.

"I don't think so," Beth said. "There's a chill in the air."

"Then I'll stay here with you," Amy said.

"No, don't," Beth said. "I know how much you like to get out of the school building. Go have lunch outdoors without me."

"Are you sure?"

Beth nodded. "I won't be here at school much longer," she said. "You had better get into the habit of eating lunch without me."

Amy smiled at her older sister. "We'll walk home together," she said. "I promise."

"I know you'll try," Beth said. "Now go, and find some friends to eat with."

Amy left Beth behind and went outside. The weather had turned cooler, but to her mind it was a perfect day to sit on the grass and eat every morsel of Hannah's delicious turnover. She made herself comfortable, and was surprised when Jenny and Susie walked over.

"We saw you sitting all alone," Jenny said. "You don't mind if we join you, do you, Amy?"

"No, of course not," Amy said. It had been so lovely when she'd been able to imagine drawing lessons for herself and Diana. But now her hopes of such lessons lay once more with Jenny, and Amy was determined to do all she could to get Jenny to ask her.

"Where's Beth?" Susie asked.

"Inside," Amy replied. "I don't always eat lunch with her."

"No, of course not," Jenny said. "It's just that we're glad you're having lunch with us instead. We were just talking about you, as a matter of fact."

"What were you saying?" Amy asked.

"All sorts of nice things," Jenny replied. "Weren't we, Susie?"

"The nicest things," Susie agreed. "How pretty you are. And talented. And friendly."

"Thank you," Amy said.

"Of course, we're not the only ones who've noticed that about you," Jenny said. "Look at Diana."

"What about Diana?" Amy asked.

"The way you and she became friends so fast," Jenny said. "She must see something very special in you also, Amy."

"Our fathers know each other," Amy replied.

"Everyone knows your father," Jenny said. "He's such a fine man. My father was speaking of him just the other day, saying what an honorable man Mr. March is."

"He's an idealist," Susie said. "That's what my father says about him."

"But a good idealist," Jenny said. "An honorable one."

"Oh, yes," Susie said. "The very best sort of idealist, I'm sure."

"So there must be another reason why Diana has chosen you for her friend," Jenny said. "Besides your father, I mean."

"Perhaps it's because I'm so pretty and talented and friendly," Amy said.

"Perhaps," Jenny said. "Or maybe Diana sees something more than that about you."

"What more could there be?" Amy asked. She took a bite of Hannah's turnover and waited for Jenny's reply. But Jenny merely smiled.

"Did you visit her on Saturday?" Susie asked instead. "Did you see Diana's house?"

Amy took another bite and nodded.

"Was it beautiful?" Susie asked. "Was it filled with wonderful things?"

Amy nodded again. She hoped she could make Hannah's turnover last through the lunch period so that she wouldn't have to reply.

"I should so love to see it," Susie said. "I think you must be the luckiest girl in Concord, to be so friendly with Diana."

"Diana does seem very sweet," Jenny said. "Is she as kind at home as she is in school?"

That seemed safe enough to answer. "Yes, she is," Amy said. "She even offered me a beautiful necklace. But of course I said no."

"Why?" Susie asked. "I'm sure if Diana had offered it to me, I would have accepted."

Amy looked at Susie. She knew Susie probably would have accepted the gift, but then Susie could easily give Diana something of equal value in return, whereas Amy could not. "I didn't think my mother would want me to accept it," Amy finally said.

"I know how it is with mothers," Jenny declared. "The way my mother goes on and on about all those lessons she makes my sisters and me take. I couldn't help noticing how interested you were in those lessons, Amy."

"I should love art lessons," Amy said. "You're very fortunate to have them."

"Fortune is meant to be shared," Jenny said. "Perhaps someday you'll consent to visit me and take art lessons by my side."

"I'd like that very much," Amy said, hardly daring to believe that Jenny was extending an invitation.

"Of course I shall have to ask Mama," Jenny said. "But I'm sure she'd approve."

"Thank you," Amy said. "It would mean the world to me to take art lessons."

"I never realized you wanted them so much," Jenny said. "If they're that important to you, Amy, I'm sure you'd be willing to do a small thing for me."

"Of course," Amy said. "What is it, Jenny?"

"It's nothing, really," Jenny said. "Susie and I would simply like you to settle a wager we've made."

"A wager?" Amy asked. "My family doesn't approve of gambling."

Jenny laughed. "Not that sort of wager. Is it, Susie?"

"No," Susie said, but she looked as bewildered as Amy felt.

"It's simply that Susie has one theory about Diana, and I have another," Jenny said. "Things we've heard, if you know what I mean. And since you've been to her home, we're sure you'll know the answer."

Amy took another bite of her turnover.

"Susie says the reason Diana isn't allowed to have callers is that her father really doesn't have any money," Jenny said. "But I've heard there's something the matter with her brother. I've heard he's a monster boy, that his body is all twisted and diseased. Which is it, Amy?"

"Neither," Amy said. "Diana's house was filled with treasures, and I met her brother and he's perfectly healthy."

"Then what could it be?" Jenny asked. "I'm sure if you want those art lessons enough, Amy, you'll be willing to tell me what Diana's secret is."

Amy took another bite of her turnover and

thought about what she should say. It would be so easy to tell Jenny the truth. Amy owed Diana nothing. And art lessons meant everything to Amy. They might even help her earn the money her family badly needed.

After all, Diana had never confided in her. It was David who had told her, and he had acted as though the world already knew. He might even prefer it if people did know the truth about his mother, especially if everyone was saying he was a monster boy.

Jenny smiled at Amy. "My art instructor is so wonderful," she said. "I'm sure he'd enjoy teaching a girl with as much talent as you have."

"Besides, Diana would want us to know," Susie said. "How can we be her friends if we don't know what her problem is?"

Amy swallowed the last bite of her turnover. It would be so easy, she thought. And it would mean so much to her.

"Diana . . . Diana's only problem is that she doesn't like either one of you," Amy said, getting up and brushing the crumbs off her

dress. "But I can't really say that's her problem. Frankly, I think it's good taste on her part."

"What nerve!" Jenny yelled. "Don't ever expect art lessons from my instructor!"

"I never really did," Amy said. "Good-bye Jenny. Good-bye, Susie. I'll be sure to tell Diana you were asking after her." And with that, she walked away and back to her sister, who knew the truth and didn't judge.

CHAPTER 9

"*I* know I promised I'd walk home with you," Amy said to Beth when the school day had finally ended. "But I really want to go to Diana's."

"I understand, and you have good reason," Beth said. "I hope Diana didn't miss school because she's ill."

"If she is, I hope I'm not the cause," Amy said, and she gave Beth a big smile.

This time the walk to the Hugheses' home didn't seem as long. The butler answered the door and ushered Amy in. "Miss Diana is in her room," he said. "She hasn't been feeling well all day."

"I'd like to see her anyway," Amy said. "I won't stay long enough to tire her out, I promise. I know the way." She ran up the stairs before the butler had a chance to stop her.

"Diana," Amy said, knocking on the door. "It's me, Amy. May I come in?"

"Amy?" Diana said, opening the door. She was wearing the most beautiful nightdress Amy had ever seen.

"How are you feeling?" Amy asked. "I was worried about you."

"I've had a headache all day," Diana said.

"May I sit down?" Amy asked, and walked over to one of the chairs by the window. "Headaches are terrible," she said. "I get them when I worry about things."

"I do too," Diana said.

"It isn't fair you should have to worry about anything," Amy said. "What's the point of being rich and beautiful if you still have to worry?"

"Nobody's life is perfect," Diana said. "Least of all mine."

"That's one reason why I came to see you,"

Amy said. "To tell you I don't care if your life isn't perfect. I mean, I wish it were. I wish my life were. But I don't think less of you because your life isn't, any more than you'd think less of me because my life isn't. Which it isn't, if you know what I mean."

"I think I do," Diana said. "And it's very sweet of you to come here to tell me that."

"I'm not sweet," Amy said. "Any more than I'm modest. But I like you, Diana, and I hope you like me. Not just because my aunt March says I'm respectable, but because of who I am. Me. Amy March."

"Oh, I do," Diana said. "I've liked you since the moment you walked up to me at school. And I had no idea who you were then."

"Fine," Amy said. "Because I want to talk honestly, and I'm not sure you'll like me so much after I'm through."

Diana sat down on her bed. "You think I'm wicked, don't you?" she said. "Because of my mother. I understand if you do."

"I don't feel that way at all," Amy said. "I

don't care who your mother is or what she's done. My sister Jo has done some really wild things, running around and making a spectacle of herself, and if I thought people were going to judge me by her behavior, I would simply die. Or at least I'd leave Concord and never show my face here again."

"It's not quite the same thing," Diana said. "My mother has brought shame to my entire family."

"What your mother did was sinful," Amy said. "And I'm sorry for you and your family. But I don't like you any less because of it. It's like Hannah's turnover."

"What does Hannah's turnover have to do with this?" Diana asked.

"That's what I have for lunch every day," Amy explained. "Because they're cheap and they're filling. And *you* have a wonderful lunch every day. But you don't like me any less because all I have is Hannah's turnover, now, do you, Diana?"

"No, of course not," Diana replied.

"You see," Amy said. "There are people who think my father is a terrible man because he chose not to go into business. And now that he's left us to be a chaplain, some people think even worse of him. Don't deny it. My aunt March is one of them, so I know it's true. But Aunt March doesn't think I'm a terrible person because Father's become a chaplain. She likes me. I even think she likes Jo, although I can't imagine why."

"I don't think being poor is quite the same as being fallen," Diana said.

"I'm not so sure," said Amy. "I know there are girls who aren't my friends just because I don't have money. And maybe they won't be your friends because of your mother. We'll both be judged because of our parents."

"But I may never be able to marry a respectable man," Diana said. "I know my father worries fearfully about that."

"I probably won't marry a wealthy one," Amy said. "And I would so love to. It really isn't fair what our parents do to us, Diana."

"No," Diana said. "It really isn't."

"That's one reason why I came," Amy said. "But there are others. How is your headache?"

"Better, I think," Diana replied.

"I'm going to make it worse, I'm afraid," Amy said. "Diana, I told my sisters about your mother."

"Is that all?" Diana asked.

"Isn't that enough?" Amy said.

Diana laughed. "I thought you were going to say something far worse," she answered. "That we could never be friends, or something like that."

"I walked all the way over here to tell you we *are* friends," Amy said. "But if you're angry at me because I told my sisters, I'll understand. I just felt you had the right to know."

"I knew you'd tell them," Diana said. "You probably tell them everything."

"Just about," Amy agreed.

"Have you told anyone else?" Diana asked.

Amy shook her head. "Jenny and Susie

tried to find out why your father doesn't want you to have callers," she said. "I told them you didn't like them. I hope you don't mind."

"Not at all," Diana said. "They're nasty girls."

"Yes, they are," Amy said, knowing she'd never have private art lessons and feeling terribly sorry for herself. Why couldn't it have been Jenny's mother who ran off with the riding instructor and Diana's mother who insisted on art lessons? Life was completely unfair. "Oh," Amy said, "that reminds me. You're not still angry at David, are you?"

"No," Diana said. "I know I said terrible things to him, but I apologized that evening."

"I say the same and worse to Jo all the time," Amy said. "Is David in? There's something he should know."

"He's out with his tutor," Diana replied. "Could I tell him instead?"

"I think you had better." Amy sat up straight. "There's a rumor going around that he's some kind of monster boy. Diseased and deformed. I think it would be good if he got around more, went to town, introduced himself to others. He could start by coming to my house. He's just about Jo's age, and she knows lots of other people. We could have a party."

"A party?" Diana asked.

"Not a fancy one," Amy said. "But the weather's so nice now, we could certainly have a picnic. And Jo could put on one of her plays. They're really very good, especially now that I'm big enough to play the important parts."

Diana laughed. "You're right," she said. "You're not modest, Amy."

Amy blushed, but then she laughed too. "Do say you'll come. You and David both."

"We'd love to," Diana said. "David's been as lonely as I have the past few years. And I know Father would approve. Oh, thank you, Amy."

"You're very welcome," Amy said, getting up from her chair. "Now, if your headache is better, could you show me the rest of your things? I never got to see your dresses, and I would so love to."

"They're right in here," Diana said, opening the armoire. "Tell me which one you think I should wear when I meet Meg and Jo for the first time."

"Any one would do," Amy said. "They really wouldn't care." And as she said it, Amy knew just how fortunate she was to have a family who knew that love was important and social position wasn't. "Dress however you want, Diana. It won't matter at all."

PORTRAITS OF LITTLE WOMEN ACTIVITIES

MACE AND RAISIN
COFFEE CAKE

Coffee cakes have always been popular, probably because they are so good to eat. Everyone seems to have a special way of making them, adding this or that ingredient. The mace in this old-fashioned recipe will fill your kitchen with a wonderful aroma!

INGREDIENTS
  ½ cup butter, melted and cooled
  1 cup sugar
  3 eggs
  2 cups flour
  2 teaspoons baking powder
  1 teaspoon mace

¼ teaspoon salt
1¼ cup milk
1½ cups chopped raisins

Preheat oven to 350 degrees.
1. Add melted butter to sugar in a bowl and mix well.
2. Add eggs to butter-sugar mixture and blend in thoroughly.
3. In another bowl, mix together flour, baking powder, mace, and salt. Add to egg mixture, alternating with milk. Blend with a wooden spoon.
4. Mix in raisins.
5. Grease a 9-by-13-inch baking pan and pour in cake mixture.
6. Bake about one hour, or until center is dry. (To test, insert knife and pull out.) Let cool before removing from pan.

This is delicious served with vanilla ice cream.

CITRUS - CINNAMON POTPOURRI

Whether in a lovely glass jar covered with lace, or in lace all by itself, this potpourri will make any room, closet, or dresser drawer wonderfully fragrant.

MATERIALS

- 3 oranges
- 3 lemons
- 3 limes
- 4 cinnamon sticks, coarsely crushed
- 3 whole nutmegs
- 8 whole allspice
- 3 bay leaves, halved
- Clear glass jar, to hold about 6 ounces
- 6-inch round of lace to cover jar
- *Or:* Instead of jar, 12-inch round of lace to hold potpourri
- Ribbon, about ½ yard long and ½ inch wide

CITRUS-CINNAMON POTPOURRI

① Using a vegetable peeler, peel the skins (not the white pith) from the fruits.

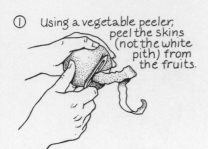

Skins are dry when they snap in your fingers.

② Simmer skins in water until they're translucent (about ½ hour).

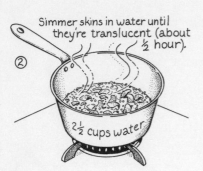

2½ cups water

④ Add 4 cinnamon sticks (coarsely crushed)

3 whole nutmegs

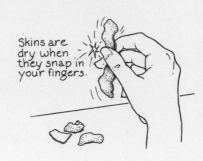

8 whole allspice

3 bay leaves (halved)

③ Drain skins, then spread them on a cookie sheet covered with parchment or foil.

Dry in oven at 150° to 175° for about 2 hours.

Toss all items by hand.

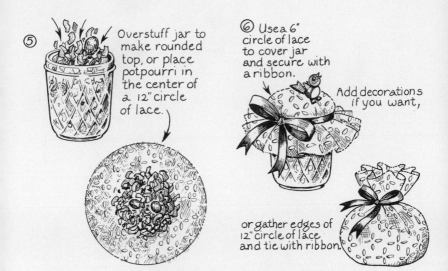

⑤ Overstuff jar to make rounded top, or place potpourri in the center of a 12" circle of lace.

⑥ Use a 6" circle of lace to cover jar and secure with a ribbon.

Add decorations if you want,

or gather edges of 12" circle of lace and tie with ribbon.

The aroma of this potpourri will last a long time. Shake it now and then to renew the fragrance.

ABOUT THE AUTHOR OF
PORTRAITS OF LITTLE WOMEN

SUSAN BETH PFEFFER is the author of both middle-grade and young adult fiction. Her middle-grade novels include *Nobody's Daughter* and its companion, *Justice for Emily*. Her highly praised *The Year Without Michael* is an ALA Best Book for Young Adults, an ALA YALSA Best of the Best, and a *Publishers Weekly* Best Book of the Year. Her novels for young adults include *Twice Taken*, *Most Precious Blood*, *About David*, and *Family of Strangers*. Susan Beth Pfeffer lives in Middletown, New York.

A WORD ABOUT
LOUISA MAY ALCOTT

LOUISA MAY ALCOTT was born in 1832 in Germantown, Pennsylvania, and grew up in the Boston-Concord area of Massachusetts. She received her early education from her father, Bronson Alcott, a renowned educator and writer, who eventually left teaching to study philosophy. To supplement the family income, Louisa worked as a teacher, a household servant, and a seamstress, and she wrote stories as well as poems for newspapers and magazines. In 1868 she published the first volume of *Little Women*, a novel about four sisters growing up in a small New England town during the Civil War. The immediate success of *Little Women* made Louisa May Alcott a celebrated writer, and the novel remains one of today's best-loved books. Alcott wrote until her death in 1888.